THUNDER

Junior Park Ranger

Volume 1: Vicksburg National Military Park

From your friends at
Amboy United Methodist Church

Stormy Miller

Trish Madell

The Maine Mediator Press

Illustrations and Layout by Erick Sulaiman

ISBN-13: 978-0-9991718-0-6

INTRODUCTION

The National Military Park in Vicksburg, Mississippi, preserves the historic battlefields of the most epic campaign fought in the Western theater of the American Civil War. But this book is not a Civil War story; instead, it tells the story of how the park continues to serve the community today while maintaining its trust to preserve the historical facts and artifacts of the great battle and siege.

In the spring of 2011, melting snow and ice from a harsh winter combined with heavy spring rain to bring a five-hundred-year flood to the lower Mississippi River basin. In addition to the many people displaced by the floodwater, hundreds of animals were forced to leave their homes and seek higher ground. Many of those animals were lucky enough to find their way to the Vicksburg National Military Park—1,800 acres of woods and meadows in the middle of the famed fortress city that sits atop a high bluff overlooking the river...

CHAPTER 1

As a junior park ranger, I get to live in national parks and help the other rangers protect and preserve beautiful and unique natural landscapes and important historic places. It's our job to make sure that future generations have the parks to enjoy just as we enjoy them now. It's a great job.

A lot of other animals live in national parks too. Rangers help protect them by preserving their habitats. You probably know that a habitat is a place where animals like to live because they can find food and shelter and can be safe there. I really like helping the other animals in the park.

I bet you're wondering how I got a great job like this. It all started back on the South Texas farm where I was born. It's beautiful country down there, orange-growing country. On our farm, there were lots of orange trees and lots of orange dogs. You see, I'm a Vizsla—my whole family are Vizslas—and Vizslas are kind of an orangey-red color all over. As for the orange trees, they were fruit trees full of colorful round oranges that look just like bouncy balls. As a young pup, I used to love to jump up and grab a fun toy or a tasty snack right off the tree. Pulling oranges off the tree was one of my favorite things to do.

I lived on the farm with my mama Rubi, my grandma Tiara, my aunt Groovy, my cousin Nikki, and my four little sisters. I love my family...but that's a lot of girls for one pup to put up with. My little sisters were always wanting to play Barbies or dress-up or have a big dance party. But I'd rather play ducks—that's a game where someone grabs a squeaky duck by the tail and throws it as far as they can, and then I run after it and bring it back. Then we have a duck tug of war until somebody gives up. You don't dress the duck up in doll clothes or brush its hair or any of that stuff—you just grab him by the tail and fling him. It's a fun game.

Mama and Aunt Groovy liked to go shopping and pick out cute little outfits for me. When they got home, they always wanted me to try the outfits on and have a fashion show for my grandma. Then my grandma would start hugging and kissing me and telling me what an adorable little gentleman I was. I think that's how I became such a fast runner—I was always running away from somebody who wanted to paint my toenails or tie a bow on my collar.

Then one day Ranger Mike came to our farm for a visit. I liked him a lot. We played and played and had so much fun that Ranger Mike asked if I wanted to come with him to Mississippi to be a Junior Park Ranger.

"You bet I want to go!" I said, and I ran out to tell my mom, Rubi, and all the girls.

Mama packed my favorite squeaky duck and my tennis balls in a bag with some kibble and some puppy treats for the road. She said, "I love you, Thunder, and I'm very proud of you. I know you'll be a good boy and a good Junior Ranger."

"I love you too, Mama."

"Message me when you get to Mississippi."

"I will, Mama," I promised.

Then I said goodbye to my four sisters, who were milling around us. One said, "I want to be a Junior Park Ranger too, Thunder."

And another said, "Me too, Thunder...what's a park?"

And another said, "What's a ranger?"

And the last one said, "Yeah, and what is Mississippi?"

You know, those are all good questions, I thought. Maybe I should have asked those questions myself, because now that they mention it, I don't really know either. "I don't have time to explain now, girls. I'll post some pictures when I get there," I said.

Grandma hugged me and said, "Remember, you're a pointer son, and the Southeast Texas Vizslas always perform a sharp point—that includes your tail."

"That's right," Aunt Groovy and Cousin Nikki chimed in. "Watch your tail angle."

"I will," I promised.

Then Ranger Mike opened the rear hatch on his Santa Fe and said, "Come on, Thunder. Hop in, boy."

One more quick sniff from Grandma and Mama and I hopped into the SUV fairly bursting with excitement and anticipation. "I'm off to see the world!" I said as I waved goodbye to my family and our farm.

I watched my family get smaller and smaller out of the back window as the SUV made its way down the long driveway, and I started to get a funny feeling in my tummy. The farther we went, the lower my stomach sank, and it hit bottom about the time we made it to the end of the driveway. As we turned onto the highway, I thought with panic, What am I doing? I've never been off the farm before. So what if I have to play dress up and get my toenails painted...I want my mama! And I started to wail.

"How, how, howwwwwwwwwwww! Yip, yip, yowwwwwwwwwww! Nip, nip, nowwwwwwwwwwww!"

"Don't cry little guy," said Ranger Mike. "We'll have lots of fun at the park." I sniffed a couple of times, and then Ranger Mike put me up in the front seat and gave me a puppy treat. He rolled down the window so I could see and smell all the new exciting scenery as we drove along, and I started to feel better. I began to look forward to seeing my new home.

***

"The city of Vicksburg is called the key to the South because it sits three hundred feet high on a bluff overlooking the Mississippi River," Ranger Mike explained when we arrived late that afternoon. "A very important part of the Civil War happened right here in Vicksburg, and the park preserves the historic battlefields. All of these monuments, cannons, and the ground itself tell the story of the epic battle and siege that happened a hundred fifty years ago."

Ranger Mike stopped at a place where you could look out from on top of the bluffs and see where the Yazoo River flowed into the Mississippi River and a wide vista of the surrounding countryside. We got out of the car and walked over to the edge for a better view. Down the steep hillside below sat a huge boat—but not an ordinary boat. It was an ironclad gunboat from the Civil War. Ranger Mike said, "This boat is called the Cairo, and it is the only ironclad preserved and on display anywhere in the world," he said. I wagged my tail with interest, so he continued to tell me the story. "The boat went down in the Yazoo River on her very first mission, when her Captain tried to sneak past the long row of cannons that sat here on the high ground aimed down at the river. All the sailors were able to swim to shore, but the boat sank and lay half buried in the muddy river bottom, all but forgotten for over a hundred years until a park historian identified its location and led a huge recovery effort."

We got back in the car and drove down the hill past the Cairo and past the beautiful green terraced lawn of the National Cemetery. Ranger Mike said, "Many soldiers from the Civil War are buried here in Vicksburg—and even one camel. The camel's name was Douglas, and his job was to carry the band instruments for his unit of the

Mississippi infantry. All the soldiers liked him so much that he became their mascot, but he fell in battle like many other soldiers and was buried alongside them with full military honors." A little farther down the road, Ranger Mike pulled into the driveway of a cute little white house.

"Here we are, Thunder. This is your new home," he said.

CHAPTER 2

We got out of the car and ambled over to the front door. I saw it had a second little door cut into the bottom. I gave it a sniff. Hmmm, that door must be for junior rangers to use, I figured, so I nudged it open with my nose and walked right inside. Ranger Mike came in through the big door and showed me a nice, comfy bed over by the window, all made up and ready for me. Then he set out a large bowl of water and assured me that he had plenty of kibble on hand, so I unpacked my squeaky duck and my tennis balls and made myself at home right away.

But I soon realized there was something else inside the house, something mysterious and creepy. I caught a brief glimpse of it lurking in the shadows, but a second later it was gone. It moved without making a sound, appeared out of nowhere, and then vanished without a trace. It sent a shiver up my spine to think about it. A ghost? No, a ghost I could deal with; a ghost might even be interesting…it was much worse than that.

The first time I got a really good look at the creature, I naturally assumed there had been a home invasion while Ranger Mike was picking me up down in Texas. I wasted no time—after all I was here to help—so I spoke right up. "Cat!" I said. "Cat, Ranger Mike, cat!" But Ranger Mike didn't seem to understand. So I pointed at her; after all, Vizslas are pointers. I executed several sharp points at the feline, but still Ranger Mike did nothing to shoo the intruder from the premises.

Later, after Ranger Mike poured kibble into a bowl for me, he took a small, funny-looking can down from the cupboard. When he opened the can, it smelled horrible, but he put it into a bowl on the floor and said, "Here you go, Spot." That's when it hit me. Ranger Mike has a cat.

Now, don't you think if you were going to invite someone to move in with you and offer them a swell job as a junior ranger, you would mention you share your quarters with a cat? Well, he didn't mention it, not a single word. But my mama, Rubi, raised us pups to be flexible—you know, to point and retrieve—so I was sure I could adapt to the living arrangements.

After dinner, we watched TV for a little while. I sat on the floor, and Spot curled up in Ranger Mike's lap. She was a small cat as near as I could judge, not having a lot of experience with the species. Her smooth white coat was contrasted by black ears, a black tail, and a single perfectly round black spot on her right hip. I guess that's where she got her name.

A few minutes later Ranger Mike said goodnight and went to bed. The cat strolled over to the window sill, climbed up, and curled her tail tightly around her spotted hip. Then she stared at me with her weird greenish-yellow eyes. It was a little creepy. I looked out the other window for a few minutes, but when I turned back, she was still staring at me. I walked over to my new bed and curled up with my squeaky duck. I closed my eyes and pretended to be asleep, but when I opened them again, she was still staring at me. I tried not to think about it, but it was no use. I couldn't sleep. I picked up my squeaky duck and padded quietly into Ranger Mike's room. I stood by the bed in the dark and looked at him until he opened his eyes. "It's dark, my mama isn't here, and that mean kitty is staring at me," I whined.

"Come on up, pup," he said.

* * *

The next day Ranger Mike and I woke up early and went for a long walk around the park. I learned that much of the terrain is very rugged, consisting of high ridges divided by deep ravines. The hillsides leading up to the ridges and down to the ravines are very steep and treacherous to walk, but this unique landscape also contributes to the natural beauty of the place. There are wide expanses of grass-covered hills where the sun beats down on the ground all day and other areas where the woods are so lush and thick with vine-covered trees that it stays cool and shady all the time.

On our walk, I discovered many of the large state monuments contain magnificent art pieces carved from stone or cast in bronze. The grandest is the Illinois monument. Its huge staircase leads to a circular room with a white marble dome topped by a gold eagle. Inside the walls are inscribed with the name of every soldier from Illinois who fought at Vicksburg.

We had been out for quite a while enjoying our walk when Ranger Mike stopped to talk to some visitors. I started to get a little antsy. After all, I hadn't done any business since we left the yard that morning. So I started sniffing around the white marble stairs of the Illinois monument. It was a pretty enticing sniff, and I was just getting ready to add my mark to the complex aroma of smells already present when I heard Ranger Mike say, "No!"

I dropped my leg to my side, bewildered. He walked over and said to me, "Thunder, we do not go on the monuments here in the park. There are plenty of trees and bushes and acres and acres of grass. Choose any other place you like, but we don't go on the monuments."

"Right," I barked. "You can count on me."

Later that afternoon, Ranger Mike helped me Skype with my mama and the girls. I was fine, but I'm sure they were missing me pretty bad by now. On the screen, I could see my mama and my grandma smiling at me, and in the background, I could see my four little sisters wearing fluffy pink tutus. They were standing very straight on their hind paws with heads held high, jumping, spinning, and daintily walking in tiny little steps on the tips of their paws.

"Hey, Mama! Hey, Grandma. Hey, girls. What's going on there?" I asked.

"Hello, Thunder," Mama said. "I signed the girls up for ballet classes. I was going to sign all five of you pups up before you decided to go with Ranger Mike to be a junior park ranger."

Yikes, I thought, Ranger Mike came just in time. But to my mama I said, "I'm sure the girls will love it."

Mama said, "Tell us about your new home, Thunder."

"Well, the park is beautiful and exciting with plenty of places for a bird dog like me to do some pointing. I'm already learning to be a junior ranger too, Mama. I learned the number one rule in the park is don't pee on the monuments!"

"That's wonderful, son," my mama said. "I'm so proud of you, and I love you very much."

It made me feel so good for Mama to say she was proud of me. Now I am more determined than ever to become a good junior ranger. "Thank you, Mama," I said. "I love you too."

Just then I heard the unmistakable sound of kibble hitting the bottom of a stainless steel bowl. "I have to go now...dinner is on. Love you, Grandma, and give my love to all the girls."

CHAPTER 3

Over the next couple of weeks, I rode with Ranger Mike on his rounds and started to learn the routine. This morning seemed no different at first. It was a beautiful spring morning with a clear blue sky and a few fluffy white clouds. Ranger Mike and I left early to make our rounds of the park tour road just like we do every morning. We started at the Visitor Center parking lot and then drove through the arch and down Union Street. We had just passed the Minnesota monument when we got a call on the radio from the maintenance crew asking us to come to the Illinois monument right away. "We're almost there," Ranger Mike answered into the radio. We rounded the curve and the Illinois came into view. We could see the crew alongside the tour road looking at something on the ground.

"What's up?" Ranger Mike asked as we hopped out of the truck.

Ken, the crew leader, pointed to a large area of uprooted turf. "This wasn't here yesterday," he said with concern. "This whole patch of grass was

17

torn out overnight. We've got a serious problem on our hands, Ranger Mike. Once the grass is gone, soil washes away a little bit every time it rains, and it's difficult to get new grass to grow fast enough to prevent erosion."

Then Ranger Mike said, "Burrowing like this in small patches is nothing new. Armadillos turn over patches of turf like this looking for grubs and bugs to eat, and we have a few of them in the park. But a large patch appearing overnight…it would take an army of armadillos to do that kind of damage."

"Or one giant armadillo," Ken said, and they all laughed. But I didn't get why they were laughing. If we have a giant armadillo roaming the park all night shredding up the grass, that's not funny—it's serious! I decided I had better take the lead on finding the oversized offender.

***

We returned to the visitor's center in time for the morning cannon fire. The cannon crew fires a cannon every morning at 11 a.m. sharp so all our visitors can get an idea of how loud artillery fire sounds. Ranger Mike and I were standing by while the cannon crew put a blank powder charge in the cannon barrel and then used the long-handled tamping rod to tamp it down.

As we watched the cannon crew, I was also keeping my eye on a big schnauzer who had just hopped out of a car at the far end of the parking lot. I didn't like the way he was sniffing around the 151st Ohio cavalry monument. He sniffed and circled a couple of times, and then he sniffed all along the base of the monument. I know what's going on here, I thought. He's about to violate rule number one: Don't pee on the monuments! Not on my watch! I fired a warning bark in his direction, "Woof! Woof! Woof! Woof! Woof!" Then I charged over to him. "Don't lift that leg, sir! We do not go on the monuments here in the park."

"Maybe you don't," said the schnauzer, "but I sniffed around this whole area, and I assure you, this spot is the prime for a drop or two. Now stand back, youngster, and let me take aim."

"Hey, who are you calling youngster? I am operating in my official capacity as an official junior ranger. Now, how about a little respect for the badge that I don't exactly have yet but hope to someday earn?" He inched closer to the granite memorial. "Back away from the monument, schnauzer," I warned. "Keep it dry…not a single sprinkle."

"Who's gonna stop me, Deputy Dog?" he said as he slowly cocked his leg.

"Okay, if that's how you want to play it... just remember you asked for this." Then I began to count down out loud: "Five, four, three..." Because I'm here every day, I knew what was about to happen. "Two, one."

Just then the sergeant yelled, "Fire!" The corporal pulled the lanyard setting off the charge inside the cannon with a colossal boom. The visitors reacted as always with surprise, applause, and even a few squeals. But the schnauzer jumped at least three feet straight up, right out of his skin, as we say down in Texas. I bet he knows I'm an official junior ranger now.

CHAPTER 4

After lunch, Ranger Mike had paperwork to do, so I decided to get right to work looking for the giant armadillo. Catching it could be my chance to show Ranger Mike what a valuable addition I was to the team. I headed back over to the Illinois monument and set up a stakeout, hoping to catch the enormous culprit in the act.

I backed myself into some underbrush along the edge of the clearing so I would be camouflaged. From there, I had a good view of the churned-up turf. I kept a vigilant watch for a while, but not much was happening under the bright afternoon sun, and I felt my eyelids getting kind of heavy. I must have dozed there for hours until sounds of rustling and scratching roused me. I jumped up and start sniffing around. I heard it again, rustling and scratching over in the bushes on the edge of the woods.

The underbrush here is thick, and a layer of leafy green ivy bridges the gap between it and the treetops. Anything could be hiding back there in the shadows behind those vines and bushes. I reacted instinctively, freezing into a perfect point and not moving a single muscle. Then slowly, ever so slowly, I began to creep up on the bushes. Steady, Thunder, don't give yourself away, I was thinking. Then I caught a glimpse of white fur in the shadows. White fur? I only knew one animal around here with white fur, and that was Spot. She must be spying on my operation...and just when I was trying to impress Ranger Mike. "Out of there, kitty cat," I said as I poked my face under the bushes.

Boy, was I surprised when it was not a mostly white kitty with a little black fur but a mostly black critter with a little white fur. "I–I beg your pardon," I stammered. "I thought you were somebody else." He turned to run, and I got a good look at his tail right in my face. "Wait! I want to ask you a question," I said. But he kept moving, so before I even realized what I was doing, I reached out and carefully snagged the little fellow by the tail. Immediately I regretted that action as something indescribably vile exploded in my mouth. I let go and started hacking and coughing, wiping my tongue on the grass as I tried to get that awful taste out of my mouth. That's when I noticed the smell. It saturated the air instantly with a stench so strong it was disorienting.

I had to get away from that smell! I ran to the right... I ran to the left... I ran around in circles for a minute or two... but there was no escape. The smell was all over me.

I plodded back to the ranger station with a pretty good idea of what would happen next, and I was not disappointed. After numerous pee-ews from the other rangers, Ranger Mike produced a big tub and a gallon jug of Skunk Off shampoo. "Don't worry, buddy. I've got you covered," he said sympathetically. Then he filled the tub with water, and I stepped in. It took a little time and a lot of scrubbing, but eventually I began to smell like a dog again.

After my bath, Ranger Mike and I headed home for the evening. We walked inside the house, and I flopped down in my favorite place in front of the kibble bin to wait for dinner time.

There was no sign of the cat so far, and that was always good news, but I still had kind of an eerie feeling that I was being watched. You never know where she might be; she can levitate to uncanny heights and bend herself into contorted, unnatural positions. I surveyed the room. There she was on top of the refrigerator, staring down at me like a turkey buzzard on a dead tree limb. I tried unsuccessfully to suppress a shudder.

"Smells like you made a new friend," she meowed.

"How do you know about that?" I asked. "The label on the shampoo bottle claimed "Gets rid of all the skunk smell so no one will know you were skunked.""

"I'm not sure that shampoo is living up to its advertising claims," she sneered.

Great, I thought, if she can still smell me, everyone else can too. I went back into the living room and curled up on my bed.

Wait a minute... where's my squeaky duck? I nosed around in all the corners of my bed—no duck. I got up and looked to make sure I wasn't laying on top of him. I looked under the sofa and coffee table and finally in all the corners of the room—no duck. Hmmm, I thought, when was the last time Ranger Mike and I played ducks? It was last night after dinner, right here in this room. I remembered because Ranger Mike sat down on the sofa and then Spot came over and curled up in his lap. Then I got my squeaky duck and brought it over to him, and he said, "You want to play ducks, boy?" Then he put Spot down on the floor, she sulked away and Ranger Mike played ducks with me right here in this room. He should still be here, what could have happened to him? I was thinking when I heard Ranger Mike pouring out my kibble for dinner. Finally, I thought. I'll eat dinner and look for my duck again later.

After dinner, I expanded the search area to include the rest of the house. In the bedroom, I looked under the bed, under the covers, and through a pile of dirty laundry I found on the closet floor. I searched in the bathroom, the linen closet, and the laundry hamper. I moved on to the kitchen, looking behind the trash can and under the table. I could see Spot back on her new favorite roost atop the fridge.

"What's the matter?" she said. "Can't find your dolly?"

"It's not a doll. It's a lifelike, synthetic migratory water fowl," I said indignantly. "It provides fun and realistic play for pointing and retrieving breeds."

She sneered down at me. "You're a pointer; I can vouch for that."

"You hid my duck!" I accused. "Tell me where it is right now."

"No," she purred contemptuously, but then she nudged something, moving it closer to the edge of the top of the fridge. The very tip of the duck's tail feathers became just visible.

"That's my duck! Give me back my duck," I said angrily. "That was mean to take my duck, you big bully. I'm just a puppy." I was so frustrated that I was shaking from nose to tail and so angry that all I could do was sputter incomprehensibly when I tried to speak. Finally, I managed to blurt out, "Bad kitty!" Then I turned and walked out with as much dignity as I could muster. I found Ranger Mike and lay down at his feet, resting my head on his shoe. Bad kitty, I thought.

CHAPTER 5

Ranger Mike said that I was pretty green, so a few days earlier he enrolled me in the Vicksburg Canine Academy. I don't really know what he means by green—I'm rust colored like all Vizslas—but it sounded like a great school, and I was excited that classes start tonight.

I was looking forward to meeting some of my colleagues from the local professional dog community. My fellow students would probably be police and military dogs, search and rescue dogs, and possibly some private security dogs—the kind that work for the Secret Service guarding the President or serve as bodyguards for rock stars.

I bet they were going to teach us hand-to-paw combat techniques, some stealthy ninja moves, and how to pick a lock with your toenail. We'd practice jumping out of airplanes with a parachute and leaping onto a helicopter as it flew away. I hoped they would get video of that last one; I'd love to send my mama a video of me clinging to a helicopter as it flew away, preferably in slow motion.

I must say, I was a bit surprised when

we arrived at the city picnic pavilion. Was this where the Canine Academy held classes? As we approached, I could see some of the other dogs gathered around the picnic tables. It was a little more of a mixed group than I had expected. I saw an Australian shepherd and a border collie—Sure, that makes sense—but there was also a Chihuahua that bounced himself off the ground a little every time he barked and some poor guy in the corner with the worst haircut I'd ever seen. His pure white fur had been teased out all over his body till you could barely tell there was a dog inside. He looked exactly like a powderpuff, and if that wasn't bad enough, I thought I smelled hairspray.

I saw a big black poodle across the pavilion. He seemed friendly and had a confident, self-assured kind of look on his face, so I walked over and introduced myself. "Hello, poodle, my name is Thunder."

"Good evening, Thunder. I am Ivan," he said.

After we gave each other a good sniff, I said, "It's my first class tonight, but I can't wait to get started learning how to rappel down a cliff face and dig people out of avalanches and things like that. I hope someone is going to dress up in one of those big puffy dog-bite-proof suits. I've always wanted to take a crack at one of those suits."

"I hate to disappoint you, Thunder," said Ivan, "but I don't think we are going to be learning any of that. You see, this is obedience class."

"Obedience class!" I said incredulously. "But I'm a junior ranger."

"Don't worry, Thunder. It's pretty easy. All you have to do is stand there till someone tells you to sit, and then you sit and they give you a treat," Ivan explained.

"You mean, I'm here to learn how to sit?" I said.

"That's right," he said.

"But I already know how to sit, Ivan. I'm literally sitting right now."

"Yes, I see that you are, my friend, but did anyone give you a treat for sitting?" Ivan asked.

Well, he had a good point there. I must have sat down a couple of hundred times, and nobody ever gave me a treat for it. "Ivan," I asked "what's your job?"

"Oh, my job is very important. I bark at the mailman, and I help out in the kitchen."

"Oh, can you cook?" I asked.

"Well, no, I don't cook. I'm in maintenance, you might say. You see, when my mom spills something, I lick it up. I'm quick too, right there on the spot—no need to fetch a mop and bucket. I've got it covered," he said proudly.

Just then the Australian shepherd strolled over and introduced herself. "Hello," she said, "I'm Indigo."

"Pleased to meet you, Indigo," I said. "I'm Thunder, and this is Ivan."

"Nice to meet you," Ivan said.

"Indigo, if you don't mind me asking, what is your job?"

"Oh, I'm so glad you asked, Thunder. I have a great job! See that cute little girl over there? That's my little girl Tanisha—hi, Tanisha! I'm her nanny. I take care of her."

"Oh, like a bodyguard?"

"Well, you could say that, but mostly I nap all day until she comes home from school. Then we get out all of her stuffies, dress them up really cute, and have a photo shoot or maybe a tea party."

"A tea party?" I echoed in disbelief.

"Oh, a tea party sounds nice," said Ivan. "Tell me, do you ever spill anything? Because I have a couple of boys at home, and we would love to come over for a tea party."

"Oh, that would be lovely," said Indigo. "Let's set up a playdate."

Geez, I thought, Ivan is right. Nobody is going to be doing any rappelling around here anytime soon. Just when I felt an eye roll coming on, the instructor called the class to order, and we all lined up next to our human companions.

"Good evening, class, and welcome to the Canine Academy of Vicksburg. I am Mrs. Katz, and I will be your instructor. We will begin with the sit command. Everyone step out in front of your dog and very distinctly say, 'Sit,' and as soon as they sit, give them a treat."

Ranger Mike stepped in front of me. "Sit," he said. So I sat down, and he gave me a treat.

Hmmm, I'm beginning to see the benefits of continuing my education. I stood back up after a moment, and Ranger Mike said, "Sit." I sat down, and there came another treat. I looked over at Ivan, he was munching on a treat too; he gave me a little wink and a nod. He's right, I think. This is pretty sweet.

But as simple as it was, some of the guys seemed to be having a little trouble. Over to my right was a beagle who had yet to sit down a single time. "What's the trouble, buddy?" I said. "Just sit down, and he'll give you a treat."

"Really?" he said anxiously. "Just sit...that's it?"

"Yeah," I said, "just park yourself right there."

"Right here?" he questioned nervously.

"Yeah," I said, "plant your butt right there."

"Now?" he asked.

"Dude, you're totally overthinking this," I said.

Behind us, I heard someone mouthing off with a distinct Scottish accent. "We Scotties are a proud lot of doggies, missy, and we dona' sit when it's convenient for you. We sit when it's convenient for us ya see, and you'll no be bribing me with your wee bit o' liver. I'll be telling you when I'll be doing some sitting, missy." I looked behind me, and he said, "And what do you think you're looking at, laddie? You go ahead and sit for the man in the funny hat if you want to, but you can just keep your big pink nose out of my business."

"Sorry," I said defensively, and I turned away. I glanced over to my left. Indigo was there performing perfect sits for Tanisha even though Tanisha could barely even say, "Sit." After each trick, Indigo delicately helped herself to a treat from Tanisha's little treat pouch. Indigo smiled at me, and I think I blushed a little, but it's hard to tell if you're blushing when you're essentially red from head to tail. On her far side was a golden doodle who clearly understood the instructions but was not exactly sitting; he was doing more of a squat and hover move. "What's his problem?" I asked.

"Oh, a bee stung him on the butt earlier today, but he didn't want to miss out on the treats," Indigo informed me.

"Yikes," I exclaimed with a little involuntary wince, and then to the doodle I said, "Way to hang in there, buddy."

I glanced to my right again. The beagle looked really stressed. He was panting hard, and his tail was completely stationary. "Don't worry, pal, I'm here for you," I encouraged him. "What's your name?"

"My name?" he asked timidly.

I could feel the tiny hairs between my paw pads start to twitch. I took a deep breath. "Yeah friend, your name," I said.

"It's G–G–Gilroy," he stammered.

"It's okay, Gilroy," I said. "We're going to get through this together."

"O–O–kay," he stuttered.

"First, you've got to relax. Take a deep breath," I said.

"Now?" he asked.

"Yes! Right now...deep breath," I said, and I heard him draw some air into his chest. "Good," I said. "Now try to relax, Gilroy. Think about something pleasant."

"P–pleasant," he said.

"Right," I encouraged. "For example, where have you sniffed today? What did it smell like?"

"I–I sniffed the stop sign at the corner this morning," he said, perking up a little. "It was fascinating, lots of unfamiliar scents...I think even some hog pookie."

"That's good, Gilroy. That sounds like an interesting sniff," I encouraged.

"Oh, it was," he said.

"Feeling a little more relaxed now?" I said. "Ready to give it another try?"

"Sh–sure," he said.

"Okay," I said, "the next time your partner says, 'Sit,' you just put your butt right down on the ground."

"Okay," he said.

"Don't rush it," I coached. "Wait for him to say it…wait for it…" Then suddenly the cub scout in front of Gilroy said, "Sit."

"Now," I said, and he gently placed his bottom on the ground, tail out and everything.

"I did it!" he exclaimed as he crunched into his treat.

"Yes sir, you did, and it was outstanding," I said.

"Thanks," he said. "It felt good."

CHAPTER 6

The next day at park headquarters, Ranger Mike and I had a meeting with some men from the Army Corps of Engineers. It was a warm and sunny 80 degrees here in Mississippi, but for some reason, they were all talking about snow and ice. Their voices sounded kind of urgent too, so I tried to listen to what they were saying.

They were talking about how North Dakota, Minnesota, and some other states had set new records for snowfall this past winter, and now that it was spring, all that snow would be melting. I know that when snow melts it becomes water, but I didn't really understand how water 1,200 miles away was going to cause any problems here. I could tell it was very serious because they said even though levees are built to keep water from spilling out of the river, they had just blasted big holes in two of them.

The engineer said, "All the melting snow has filled the river with too much water. The extra water is like a big wave on the ocean; the top of the wave is higher than the water around it. When that wave is in a river, it's called a flood surge. Blasting the levees lets some of the extra water spill out, but causes many miles of farmland to be flooded. It is a drastic step we have taken so there will be less water in the river when the flood surge gets to the city. But even after letting all that water out, there will still be a flood here in Vicksburg, and it may be the biggest flood Vicksburg has ever seen."

"When do you predict the river will crest?" asked Ranger Mike.

"In about five days," he said.

Then Ranger Mike said, "We can expect to see displaced animals throughout the park over the next two or three weeks until the flood surge passes and the river goes back to normal." I wasn't sure what he meant by "displaced" animals, but it sounded serious.

After the meeting, I went out to make my rounds before heading back over to the Illinois monument to continue the stakeout for the giant armadillo. I skirted the west side of the cemetery, passed behind the Cairo, and climbed up to the high ridge that overlooks the Yazoo River just before its junction with the Mississippi River. I took in the view from here almost every day, but this day I was looking out on a completely new landscape as both rivers had spilled out over their banks and flooded the whole valley. It was impossible to tell where one river ended and the other began; there was just water everywhere. This must be what the engineer was talking about in that meeting, I thought. There was so much water trying to make its way down the river that it was spilling over the tops of the levees and going wherever it could.

I wasn't the only one taking in the view this morning. I could see a familiar-looking black and white tail about 50 yards down the ridge. I thought I should go over and offer an apology for snagging the little skunk by the tail the other day and make sure he was okay. However, since I was approaching from the rear, I approached with caution. My mama, Rubi, always said, "Spray me once, shame on you. Spray me twice, shame on me."

"Good morning, skunk," I said. "It's going to be a beautiful day."

He looked back over his shoulder. "You," he said. "Don't you have anything better to do than harass the wildlife? This is public property, and I'm a public skunk; I have every right to be here."

"Of course you do, skunk...no need to get all defensive. I just wanted to tell you I'm sorry about grabbing you up by the tail yesterday. Sometimes I get a little carried away. Will you accept my apology?"

"Well, yes, of course," said the skunk. "Sorry I had to spray you in the mouth. You might as well know it's more or less automatic when someone grabs me by the tail."

"Perfectly understandable, skunk, although my roommate, Ranger Mike, calls me 'skunk breath' now...uh, no offense. My name is Thunder, and I'm a junior park ranger here."

"It's nice to meet you, Thunder. My name is Seymour. I appreciate your apology more than you know, Thunder. The past few days have been very difficult for my mother and me."

"I'm so sorry to hear you have had trouble, Seymour. What happened?"

"Well, my mother and I had a snug little den under a big cypress tree up the river a piece near Lake Providence. The river has been filling up with more and more water lately, just like it is here. Then a couple of days ago, we were curled up in our den when suddenly the den filled with water and we were washed out. I was so scared. I reached out and happened to feel a big tree branch behind me. I grabbed hold, and I crawled up on top of it. The water was moving very fast, and the branch was spinning around and around. I held on as tightly as I could, and I started calling out for my mother. I saw her in the water a few feet away, and I hollered, "Here I am, Mama." She saw me and struggled to swim over; then she crawled up on the branch with me. We held on to each other as the branch was carried down river a long way by the strong current. The sun was setting when we reached a bend in the river where some logs had collected. The logs formed a jam that reached out into the river. It looked like our branch was going to pass by very close to the jammed logs. Mama said, 'This is our chance.' Then she grabbed me by the scruff of my neck and jumped out into the water as far as she could toward the log jam. I was scared, but my mom swam the last few feet and clawed her way up onto the logs. Then we ran across all those logs and up onto dry land."

"That must have been terrifying, Seymour. You and your mother are very brave. Where is your mother now?" I asked.

"Mama is resting under some bushes over at the edge of the woods; she's pretty exhausted from all that swimming. I came out to look for some food for us. That's what I was doing yesterday too when you grabbed me."

I said, "Let me help you find some food right now, Seymour."

I got Seymour and his mother situated in a nice quiet area of the park near the big statue

of General Grant on his horse. "There are plenty of acorn-bearing trees nearby and lots of rocks to turn over for grubs, but it is out of range of the big lawnmowers that move through to cut the grass every week or so," I told them. "I'll check in on you tomorrow," I said, and I trotted off in the direction of headquarters.

As I came around the corner about a mile from headquarters, I saw two teenaged boys, and their behavior was rather odd even for teenaged boys. They were over in the tall grass along the edge of the woods. They were dancing around, picking their knees up high, kicking their feet, and waving big sticks around. Here and there they were whacking the ground with the sticks. It looked kind of fun, and I took a few steps in their direction, thinking I might like to join in. But then I caught a glimpse of black and yellow on the ground, and I realized what was happening: A king snake was being attacked!

"Stop it!" I barked. "Drop those sticks right now." I charged over to them. "Woof! Woof, woof, woof, woof!" I said. Then I said to the snake, "Hurry, king snake! Slither away and hide in the woods while I hold them off." I managed to distract the boys long enough for the snake to make it into the woods and get out of sight. After a couple of minutes, the boys moved on and began to walk back toward town. When I was sure they were gone, I walked carefully over to the woods.

"King snake, they're gone now. Are you okay?" I asked. "Don't be scared. I'm a junior ranger. I won't hurt you." A minute or two passed, but then I heard leaves rustling a few yards away. Cautiously, a black snake with yellow speckles emerged from its hiding place under a stump in a thicket of honeysuckle vines.

"I think I'm okay," he said quietly. "They hit me a couple of times near my tail, but nothing seems to be broken. Thank you for helping me, ranger. I was scared."

"I'm just happy I came along in time to help. I don't know why those boys would be so mean. I'm glad you are not seriously hurt. I don't believe we've met...I'm Thunder," I said.

"I'm Chrisss," he hissed.

"Do you live in the park, Chrisss?"

"No, I don't live here. I live on a soybean farm near the Yazoo River. To tell you the truth, Thunder, I'm not sure exactly where I am or how I got here. I think I'm lost," he confessed sadly.

"Lost...that must feel awful. How did you get lost, Chrisss? Maybe I can help you."

"Well," Chrisss said, "I was home on the farm yesterday when I started to get a little thirsty. I have a real good job there keeping mice and rats out of the storage bins. You see, there's always some grain in the bins, even this early in the season, because it's impossible to get every single soybean out when they empty the silo. Even that small amount of food attracts mice and rats, and the farmer depends on me to keep them out. Otherwise, when we put the harvest in this fall, the mice will eat some, and then they'll make more mice and more mice, and they'll contaminate our whole harvest. We don't get a good price when our shipment is contaminated. If that happened, it would leave me, the farmer, his family, our chickens, and all the other farm animals struggling over the winter," he explained. "Oh, I also keep the other snakes, like copperheads and rattlers, away from the farmhouse. I do that part for free. It's just a bonus I throw in because I like to be helpful."

"Wow," I said. "You have a very important job."

"That's kind of you to say, Thunder, but the job does have its rewards. Those long rows of packed down dirt between the soybeans are just perfect for sunning my long, skinny body, and in late summer, when the sun is too hot, the plants are big enough to shade the ground. Plus, I get all the mice and rats I can eat. It's a pretty sweet deal."

"Sounds great," I said.

"I enjoy it there," he said with a shy smile, and then he continued, "so like I said, I was getting a little thirsty. Snakes need water like every other living thing, you know, so I went down to the river to get a drink and take a swim—it's something I do every few days. I usually swim part way across the river to the sand bar—the one that has two trees on one end and a big rock on the other. I take in some sun while I'm resting up, and then I swim back. Yesterday, I slipped into the water like always, and I swam in the usual direction, but I never came to the sand bar—it was just gone! The river looked so different and much bigger than usual. I tried to swim back to the farm, but without the sandbar for a landmark, I must have gone in the wrong direction. I just kept swimming until I finally came to some dry land. I crawled out down there at the bottom of the hill by the big boat."

"Wow, you've had a rough few days too. I met a baby skunk this morning who had been washed out of his home," I explained. "Now I know what Ranger Mike meant when he said we would probably find displaced animals around the park—

animals that were forced to leave their homes because of the flood and can't get back until the water goes down."

"That sounds like me! I've been displaced!" Chrisss said with alarm.

"It all has to do with melting snow a long way from here," I explained. "I didn't really get it when the engineer told us about the levees and the flood at the meeting this morning, but now that I've heard what happened to you and Seymour the skunk, I can put two and two together!"

"What's two and two?" Chrisss asked.

"Oh, it's four, but that's not important right now," I said. "The important thing is that I know how to help you find your way back to the soybean farm. You see, the sandbar is still there, Chrisss. It's just covered up with water right now because the whole valley is flooded. Once the flood surge passes, the water level will go down, and you'll be able to see the sandbar again."

"If I could see the sandbar, I could swim back home! When will the flood be over?" Chrisss asked excitedly.

"The engineer said the river would crest in five days, but it will take a few more days for the water to recede," I explained. "In the meantime,

Chrisss, please make yourself at home here in the park. Another king snake is always a welcome addition. Just be a little cautious where you sun yourself for your own safety. It's unfortunate, but a lot of people have a bad attitude about snakes. I'll come by tomorrow and see how you're doing."

"Thank you, Thunder. You've been a very good friend to me today. I hope someday I can return the favor."

CHAPTER 7

By the time I had Chrisss and Seymour settled in, I didn't have time to work on the stakeout for the giant armadillo before class that night. I trotted back to headquarters so Ranger Mike and I wouldn't be late.

Before class started, I told Ivan and Indigo what I had learned that morning about the coming flood, the displaced animals, and the giant armadillo that was wreaking havoc on the grass in the park. "The whole valley on the north side is flooded already. Tomorrow I'm going downtown to the riverfront to see for myself," I said.

"That sounds interesting, Thunder. Do you mind if I join you?" Ivan offered.

I agreed, and we made plans to meet downtown in the morning. Just then Mrs. Katz called the class to order. "Good evening, human and canine students. Tonight we will learn the heel command," Mrs. Katz informed the class. "A solid understanding of this command is required to walk on a leash properly." Yikes, I thought, I didn't know there was a wrong way to walk on a leash. However, I had watched Ranger Mike fill his pocket with doggie treats before we left the house, so I was taking an open-minded approach to any learning experience. "Everyone line up with your dog sitting on your left," Mrs. Katz directed. So far, so good...the whole class was lined up beautifully. "Now give the command, 'Heel,' and begin."

"Heel," said Ranger Mike.

I gave him a blank stare.

"Heel," he said again. I looked around the class—nothing was happening. Indigo and Gilroy looked at me questioningly. I shrugged. "I don't know. I'm gonna need more information," I said.

Then we noticed Ivan was on his feet. "I think 'heel' means walk," he said. "Pass it on."

"Ah, that makes sense. Let's try it," I said, and there was a general murmur of agreement.

The next time Ranger Mike said, "Heel," I started to walk forward. Ranger Mike walked forward too. That part was good, but something was still a bit off. For one thing, Ranger Mike seemed confused. "Mrs. Katz said right foot first," I offered helpfully. "No, right foot, right," I said. "That was your left foot...no, that's still your left."

As much as I wanted to help, my advice didn't seem to be appreciated. Ranger Mike apparently thought he had it all under control, but he was sputtering out instructions faster than I could possibly comply. "Thunder, wait—no, go—no, stop! Thunder, come back here. Thunder, that's too fast. Thunder, move over. Stop, Thunder, the leash is wrapped around your foot."

"It's wrapped around your foot too," I said. "Both of them."

Eventually we managed an uneasy method of forward momentum. I looked over at Indigo; she was holding her own leash in her mouth and still walking in perfect sync with Tanisha, matching her short stride: step, pause—step, pause—step, pause. They were adorable, like a couple of flower girls walking down the aisle in a wedding procession. I looked around. Everyone else seemed to be doing well and made it look easy. Some of the guys even looked as if they were floating along beside their partners, their paws barely touching the ground at all. Even Gilroy and the cub scout glided past as gracefully as if they were auditioning for Dancing with the Stars. "Way to go, Gilroy," I said and then, "Ooof." I bumped into the back of Ranger Mike's knee.

"Ow," he said, taking an awkward little skip and then stepping on my paw.

"Ow," I said.

The next day I left Ranger Mike at headquarters and headed downtown to meet Ivan at the corner of Washington and Clay. Downtown is typically a pretty quiet place, but today it was a beehive of activity.

The river looked huge, much higher and wider than it usually was. The river was being held back by the overflow levee, which is a long concrete wall that sits on top of the earthen levee. The floodgates were closed today, creating odd gaps in the beautiful murals depicting scenes of historic Vicksburg that are painted all along the wall. Policemen, firemen, and engineers from the Army Corps of Engineers' headquarters were moving hurriedly about. They were tending to lots of big generators and pumps with huge black hoses attached to them. The generators made a terrible racket, but it was clear to see they couldn't be turned off, because they were being used to suck up water that had gotten past the overflow wall and put it back on the other side.

Levee Street was already flooded, and half the bottom floor of the beautiful old train station was completely under water. I looked up the street to the right, in the direction of my house at the north end of the park. I could see the stop sign at the corner, the one Gilroy had said he had sniffed a few days before. The entire post was submerged, and only the red octagon with the word STOP was visible. It was as if the sign were making a plea for the water to stop rising. Ivan must have read my mind because he said, "Do you think the water will stop before it gets to your house, Thunder?"

"The engineer said that our house should be safe," I said. "But he said there was a good chance the woods and part of the cemetery will be flooded. I think it will too, Ivan. Look—the water is almost all the way across the street now, and the crest is still four days away. Some houses must be under water already...look at the train station!"

As we continued to observe the hectic activity, we saw the strangest sight yet. A family of deer swam past the train station to the edge of the water and walked out onto the street, right where some engineers were attaching a hose to one of the noisy electric pumps. They paused for a moment and then ran across Washington Street and up the hill behind us in the direction of the old Warren County Courthouse. Ivan and I looked at each other in shock. "They must be desperate to be moving in the daytime like that in the middle of all this noise and human activity," I said. "We have to do something to help them."

CHAPTER 8

I hadn't forgotten about the giant armadillo loose in the park, but I thought the desperate deer situation should take precedence, even over uprooted grass and potential erosion. Ivan and Indigo had agreed to meet me at headquarters that night to offer what assistance they could to the displaced animals. They were right on time and eager to help, but they were not alone. "Gilroy, what are you doing here?" I asked.

"I can help, Thunder, honest I can. I'll be quiet as a mouse. Please let me stay and help," he pleaded.

"Okay, fine," I said. "Just be sure to stay out of the way. This is official junior ranger business."

"Right," he said.

By midnight, we were waiting at the front gate. Nearby, a small herd of deer wandered out of the woods looking nervous and confused. "Hello. Welcome to the park," I said. They looked around, and then a couple of them walked over to me.

"Hello. Can you please tell me where we are?" the stag said cautiously.

"You're in the Vicksburg National Military Park, and I'm a junior park ranger," I said.

"Oh, you're a park ranger... maybe you can help us," said the stag. "A few days ago, water started flowing into our thicket. At first, we weren't that concerned, because it's happened before you know, so we kept an eye on it for a few days. But the water kept getting deeper and covering more and more of the thicket every day until we just had to move out. We couldn't take any chances. It's spring, you know, so we have some very young fawns in the herd. Would it be okay for us to stay in the park for a few days until this flood is over?" he asked.

"Of course," I said, "why don't you take your herd over to the west side through that archway and down Union Street. We've set up a temporary deer campground in some nice thickets back there with access to grazing around the 212th Cannon Brigade and the 153rd Artillery Position marker."

"I can show them the way," said Gilroy.

As the deer followed Gilroy down Union Street, another herd wandered up through the woods to the front gate. "More deer arriving—we

better send them over to the east side of the park near the Mississippi Infantry Position," I said.

"I'll show them the way," Indigo volunteered.

"Welcome," I said to the deer. "We have several other groups of displaced deer here tonight too, but don't worry—we'll find room for everyone. Indigo will show you to a nice thicket where you can rest up and graze a little while you wait out the flood." They thanked us and followed Indigo over to Confederate Street.

"Look, Thunder, more deer and a huge family of rabbits," Ivan said, pointing to the woods on the opposite end of the parking lot.

Gilroy returned to the makeshift welcome center with news. "Hey, Thunder, I smelled more hog pookie while I was showing that herd to their thicket. It was over by the Illinois monument, where the grass is all torn up."

"That's nice, Gilroy," I said, not really paying much attention to what he was saying, as I was busy showing the rabbits the campsite we had set up for smaller animals on the park map.

"Do you think it means anything?" Gilroy pressed.

"It probably means a hog pookied there," I said blankly. "Now come on, Gilroy, help me greet these visitors. The tour road is starting to back up."

Gilroy and I continued to greet animals and answer questions. In a few minutes, Indigo joined us looking concerned. She said, "Thunder, do you think there will be enough grass and food for everyone? They may be here for several days."

"That is a good question, Indigo," I said. "I never thought of that. I wonder where we can find more food if we need it."

"We can ask Jerry," Gilroy suggested.

"Jerry?" I said. "Who is Jerry?"

"Oh, he's the head squirrel," Gilroy said.

"The head squirrel?"

"Yeah," he said, "Jerry the head squirrel—everybody knows Jerry."

"Gilroy, I'm an official junior ranger. If there was a head squirrel here at the park, don't you think I would know about it?"

"Gee, I don't know, Thunder, but I was talking to some of the squirrels a little while ago on my way back from walking those deer to their campsite. They said that Jerry has them gather up all the extra nuts at the end of winter, and they store them in case of an emergency. He's right over there. You could go ask him about it." Gilroy pointed toward the far side of the visitor center building.

I walked a few steps over to where I could see around to the back side of the building. Sure enough, there was a big squirrel standing there who seemed to be coordinating efforts to find adequate temporary tree housing for a large number of displaced squirrels. He had several assistant squirrels scurrying around with checklists and clipboards. The refugee squirrels had formed an orderly line and were patiently waiting for tree assignments and rations. The whole operation was impressive.

I walked over. "Excuse me, squirrel," I said. "I'm Thunder, and I'm a junior ranger here at the park."

"Well, hello there, Thunder. Pleased as punch to meet you. I'm Jerry," he said. "I've heard some good things about you from the squirrels."

"Oh, you have?" I said, a little flattered.

"Yes sir, the squirrels tell me you are doing a fine job helping some of the animals that have been displaced by the flood," he said.

"Well, I'm doing my best," I said. I looked back over to where Gilroy, Indigo, and Ivan were interviewing another group of incoming deer. Indigo was chatting up a couple of the does, Ivan was trying unsuccessfully to refold a park map, and Gilroy was chasing a firefly. The deer were milling around aimlessly, and some were starting to sample the flowers planted by the park entrance sign. "Um, Jerry, how do you get them to stand in line like that?" I asked, gesturing at the squirrels, but he just laughed.

I changed the subject. "Jerry, I heard that you may have some extra food to help feed this crowd of evacuees."

"The squirrels and I have saved up quite a stockpile—been working on it for years. Come with me...I'll show you." He gave a curt whistle, and one of his assistants scurried over. "Take over for me here," he said, and then he led me over to the woods behind the building. After a brief hike, we emerged in a clearing where there were orderly rows of walnuts, pecans, and acorns stacked into little pyramids, just like tiny cannonballs.

"Amazing," I said. "How did you get so many?"

"Well," he said, "it's no secret the winters here in Mississippi are short and usually pretty mild. The trees here produce more nuts than we need for winter, so we squirrels gather up the extras and store them here for emergencies. My mama always said, 'Waste not, want not.'"

"My mama says that too!" I exclaimed.

"There you go," Jerry said. "Mamas know best."

Jerry said he would have his squirrel crew drop off some extra nuts in the areas I had designated for the displaced deer to graze. I thanked him, and we turned to walk back to the makeshift welcome center. That's when I noticed something I hadn't seen before. It was a big circle of black fencing, about the size of a small swimming pool, with a funny-looking gate on one side. The wire fence covered the top of the circle too, making it kind of like an outdoor room. "What is that?" I asked.

"Hog trap," he said.

"What's it for?" I asked.

"Trapping hogs," he said.

"I mean, why do we have a hog trap here?"

"Cuz we have hogs," he said. I could see this conversation was going nowhere, and I was antsy to get back to my pack, so I thanked him again and told him I would check in later.

We all worked most of the night getting the

displaced animals settled into their campsites and making sure they all had something to eat. It was hard work, but it was also fun. It felt good to be helpful, and it made the other animals feel better too. Gradually, uncertainty and fear gave way to friendly curiosity. The campers started to visit with each other, chatting about the weather and exchanging foraging tips. Groups gathered around in clearings as they told stories about past floods. It was almost like a party when the first hint of dawn sent everyone scurrying for shelter.

It was time for us dogs to get home too, so we said good night and headed for our homes. Indigo and Ivan trotted off to the left, while Gilroy and I walked around the corner and then up to the right.

"That was fun, Thunder," Gilroy said, smiling.

"It was fun," I agreed. "It makes you feel good to make someone else feel safe and happy, doesn't it?" I added.

"Yes, it does, Thunder. That's why I like my job so much," Gilroy said.

As soon as he said that, I realized I had never asked Gilroy about his job. "What is your job, Gilroy?" I asked now with sincere interest.

"Do you really want to know?" he asked,

wagging his tail a little too much to be cool.

"Yes, I do, Gilroy."

"Well," he said, swelling with pride, "it's my job to keep Connor company. Connor, he's my cub scout, he's kind of quiet, you know. He doesn't talk much, and he doesn't like a lot of loud noises, so he doesn't play with other kids that much. But he doesn't want to be alone all the time—he likes to have company and someone to play with sort of quietly, you know? His Grandpa Gilroy used to keep him company a lot, and Connor really liked his Grandpa. When his grandpa got sick and died, that's when I came to live with Connor. Now it's my job to keep him company and help him feel happy and secure. I'm really good at it too! I know because Connor named me Gilroy, after his grandpa."

"Gilroy, that is a great job," I said sincerely.

"Aw, thanks, Thunder," he said shyly. "The best part is, after I graduate from the Vicksburg Canine Academy, I get to put on a special vest to go to school with Connor and stay with him all day."

"No wonder you were so nervous that first night at the academy, Gilroy. That's a lot of responsibility."

"Yes, I couldn't let Connor down. He's too important to me," Gilroy explained.

Gilroy dropped off as we passed his house. "Night, Thunder," he said.

"G'night, Gilroy. See you at class," I said. As I walked the rest of the way to my house, I thought about shy, humble Gilroy and the important job he had at home. I remembered how I had sized up the other dogs that first night at obedience school, and I felt a little ashamed. I won't make that mistake again, I thought. You can't judge character or courage by size or appearance.

As I walked into our yard, I saw Spot bounce over the fence and approach the house from the opposite side. We arrived at the junior ranger door simultaneously. "Where have you been all night?" I asked.

"Where have you been all night?" she mocked.

"I've been out helping other animals because of the flood," I said indignantly.

"I've been out helping other animals," she mocked me again. "What's the big deal?" she added. "So there's a little flood. What's wrong? Can't you swim?"

"I can swim! Vizslas are part retriever!"

"Maybe Ranger Mike will get you a little life jacket or some floaties that say junior retriever ranger," she sneered.

"I don't need floaties! I can swim!" I said defensively.

"I don't need floaties. I can swim," she repeated.

Just then Ranger Mike opened the big door. "Oh, there you both are," he said. "Come on, Thunder...time for our rounds. And we have to check the new feral pig holding pens." Spot meowed and rubbed up against his pants leg, and he reached down to pet her. "Good morning, Spotty. What a good kitty," he said. As he walked off, a smear of white fur clung to the bottom of his pants, as usual. Spot gave me a rub too as she passed, and I shuddered with disgust. White fur must be the most effective mechanism for marking one's territory in any species.

"Don't forget to ask for those floaties," she said as I hopped into the truck. This is going to be a long day, I thought.

CHAPTER 9

On the way, Ranger Mike explained to me how the hog traps work. The gate opens for the hogs to walk into the pen, but it won't open to let the hogs back out. Since the traps are baited with lots of corn, the hogs don't usually even know they can't get back out, because they are too busy eating. As we made our rounds, we stopped to check each of the three new pig holding pens, including the one I had seen last night. All of them were empty, and the feeders were still full of corn. Disappointed, we drove on to headquarters.

I have to admit, after being up all night, I didn't get much done around the office the rest of that morning. Ranger Mike had more meetings about managing the crisis with the other rangers. I didn't feel like I really needed to attend, since I had already managed a big chunk of the crisis the night before, so I used the opportunity to get some shuteye before school that evening.

I was glad that I had rested up, because our lesson at the academy that night was very exciting! Mrs. Katz said we would be learning the commands "come" and "stay." It sounded like a sound bite from a motel commercial, but it turned out to be a really fun game. Ranger Mike would look at me and say, "Stay." Then he would walk off a little way and kind of pretend he had something to do. He'd pretend to look at something on his shoe, something in the woods, his watch, or anything but me. Meanwhile, I would stay put in that exact spot—waiting, and waiting, and waiting until I was vibrating with anticipation, literally about to explode—and then he would say, "Come," and I would rocket over to where he was standing quick as a flash and park it right in front of him. Then he would give me a treat, but it was so much fun I would have done it for free.

I could have played all night, but I had work to do back at the park. I had learned a lot about crisis management over the past few days, mainly that it required constant assessment of priorities. What that means is, I always needed to be working on the most important thing, but the most important thing might change at any time depending on what else was happening. I had been distracted from catching the giant armadillo by the more urgent needs of the displaced animals. But every day another section of grass was ripped up along the tour road or somewhere else in the park, so now that the animals were safe, I turned my attention back to catching the culprit and I recruited Ivan, Indigo, and Gilroy to help. The four of us agreed to meet at the Illinois monument the following night to continue the stakeout.

When we arrived at the Illinois monument, we sniffed around the area looking for clues. There were some interesting scents, including one identified by Gilroy as hog pookie. I'd really like to know how that boy learned so much about pigs, I thought. I was just about to ask when I heard Indigo saying something about leaving home in a hurry that evening. I looked over and saw she was sniffing in a very deliberate way around the last cannon in the Michigan artillery line.

Uh oh, I thought as I walked over to where she was sniffing. "Umm, Indigo," I whispered discreetly, "umm, it's just that it's against the rules to use the monuments for, uhh, well, you know... but pick any tree you like of course."

"Oh, of course, thank you," she said demurely.

I turned around just in time to see Ivan and Gilroy sniffing around the granite obelisk at the other end of the line. "Come on, guys, give me a break here," I said.

* * *

After everyone had found a good tree to do their business, we selected a vantage point with a good view of a large patch of churned up turf and settled in to wait for the big armor-clad offender. It was a beautiful night with the starry sky above us, soft grass beneath us, and a slightly cool breeze carrying delectable scents all around us. I looked over at Indigo; her eyes were half closed, and she had a peaceful expression on her face. The wind was moving just the very tips of her shiny black fur, which had a bluish tint in the reflected moonlight. That must be why they call her Indigo, I thought dreamily.

The next thing I knew I was being awakened by someone nudging me with their big wet snout. "What is it, Gilroy?" I mumbled, but then I jerked awake. "The stakeout! What's happening?" I whispered.

"Well after you three fell asleep, I caught a whiff of fresh hog pookie in the air," he said. "So I crept over to the edge of the ridge because, you see, the wind is blowing from off the river. I looked down, and there they were."

"Giant armadillos?"

"Hogs."

"Hogs?"

"Come see for yourself, Thunder," Gilroy urged.

I followed him over to the edge and looked down. Three big wild hogs were digging with their hooves and their snouts, uprooting the grass and leaving a muddy wake behind them. "This is a huge problem, Gilroy. We're going to have to deal with these hogs right away—and just when we were making some progress on the giant armadillo stakeout. I'm never gonna catch that armadillo..." Then it hit me. "Wait a minute, Gilroy," I said. "I think you might be on to something with all the hog pookie you've been sniffing lately. Think about it—the rangers just put out brand new hog traps. You smelled hog pookie by the stop sign, and then you smelled hog pookie again by one of the big patches of uprooted grass when you were showing those deer to their campsite. These wild hogs are about ten times the size of an armadillo, and they're rooting up grass as fast as they can. Gilroy, there is no giant armadillo—displaced hogs are causing all the damage!"

"Yeah, I think you're right, Thunder. I bet it's the hogs," Gilroy agreed.

"Good job picking up on that pig pookie clue, Gilroy. You've got a keen sniffer," I said, and Gilroy smiled sheepishly.

We looked down at the hogs. They were wallowing in the mud and dirt, right in front of the entrance to the Cairo museum. Huge tufts of grass were flying off of their mean-looking tusks in every direction. The big sow was snorting instructions at the two smaller hogs, "Delbert, dig some over closer to the big boat. Quigley, you get over there too and look for some more grubs. I've got a powerful taste for grubs. This will be a right nice wallow when we get done boys."

"Thunder, they're gonna start digging up another patch of grass!" Gilroy whispered urgently.

"Come on. We've got to stop them!" I said, and I charged down the hill with Gilroy in tow.

"Hold it," I said to the hogs. "Rooting and digging creates an erosion issue that could lead to a drainage nightmare!" The wild pigs stopped what they were doing and looked at me like I was crazy.

After staring at me for a moment, the big sow queried, "A what kind of nightmare?"

"A drainage nightmare," I said. "What I mean is, this area will become a big mud puddle every time it rains, and topsoil will be washed away," I explained.

"A big mud puddle is just what we want

here," she snorted. "We're right comfortable in the mud."

"I'm sorry, madam, but you cannot create a personal mud puddle in a public park," I said politely. "It isn't fair to the other park visitors who don't enjoy wallowing in mud."

"Who do you think you are to tell me what I can and can't do, skinny little dog?" she squealed.

"I am a junior ranger at this park," I said. "An official junior ranger."

"Oh, I didn't know you were official," she said sarcastically. "How about if I come over there and officially stomp you and your little buddy there into the mud? You might decide you enjoy wallowing in the mud," she said, taking a few steps in our direction.

"Stomp on 'em good, Ma," Quigley hollered while he and Delbert laughed.

"Woof! Woof! Woof!" We looked up to see Ivan and Indigo running down the hill, barking loudly as they came.

The pigs saw them too and stopped laughing, but they were still trying to play it cool. "I guess we better go, boys...and get some more of our kinfolk to come and help us root out a really big wallow." The three of them turned and headed back down the street toward the park entrance. "We'll be back soon with enough hogs to turn this whole park into our own personal mud puddle," the sow squealed as they disappeared around the corner.

CHAPTER 10

Indigo and Ivan skidded to a halt next to us as they reached the bottom of the hill. "What happened? Did we miss the giant armadillo?" Ivan asked with alarm. "Sorry, Thunder, we must have dozed off for a minute."

"There is no giant armadillo," I said. "Gilroy and I think the wild hogs are doing all the damage. We caught those three red-handed rooting up this area. They said they were making a mud hole here on purpose; they called it a hog wallow. I told them to leave, but they said they would be back with more hogs to make a really big wallow."

"Yeah, and they threatened to stomp Thunder and me into the mud too," said Gilroy indignantly.

"They don't sound very nice," Indigo said.

"They are not nice at all," Ivan said. "They can be very dangerous, and sometimes they attack people and dogs. Back in Russia, a wild boar attacked my family on the farm where we lived." He paused a moment. "Our farm was just outside Voronezh...not a huge farm but big enough. We grew wheat mostly, but we also had a big vegetable garden, an apple orchard, and a few goats and chickens. It was Mother's job to guard the farm, and she was very good at it, but she still made time to devote to our education. I come from a litter of nine you know, and that is a lot of puppies to manage, even for a smart and educated poodle such as my mother. That night, Mother had corralled us all into one of the empty stalls for a bedtime story. Her stories were wonderful, full of Russian history and the poodles who lived it. She was such a good storyteller that the draft horses and our heifer always listened too."

"That night, Mother was telling us the story of Yuri and his beautiful white poodle, Galicia, and how they founded the city of Moscow. Without warning, a huge wild boar appeared in the doorway of the barn, snorting and pawing the ground with his front hooves. Mother leapt up to face him, baring her teeth and growling viciously. She barked for the farmer to come right away. She and the boar were locked in a stare-down, the boar snorting and Mother growling and advancing slowly toward the wild animal. Outside, we heard the farmhouse door slam and the farmer's boots running toward the barn. But suddenly, the boar charged. Mother snapped at his snout, but he caught her in the side with one of his great tusks. The farmer burst through the door and shot the boar. Then he saw Mother bleeding on the floor and rushed to her side. My siblings and I ran over to her too. She looked at us, and smiling, she whispered, 'I'm so glad you are all safe, my puppies. Grow up happy and strong, and make wonderful lives for yourselves full of love and helpfulness'; then she was gone." Ivan's head hung down for a moment, and we were all silent as we reflected on the significance of Ivan's words and the depth of his loss.

Gilroy wiped a tear from his eye with one front paw, Indigo was sniffling, and, for once, I was at a loss for words. "I'm sorry for your loss, Ivan. Your mother must have been a very brave poodle," I finally managed to say.

"Oh, she was," said Ivan. "Do not be sad, my dear friends, because I honor my mother every day by living the happy and useful life she wished for me. Thunder, I would be honored to help you rid the park of these wild swine."

"I want to help too," said Gilroy.

"Count me in," Indigo echoed.

"Thank you, guys," I said, "but we're going to need a plan— a good plan—and I'm fresh out of ideas. The rangers already have hog traps with big holding pens in the park, but the hogs won't go into the traps—the rangers haven't caught a single pig. If we could get the hogs to go into the pens, the rangers would take care of the rest, but how are we going to get them to go into the pens?"

I looked around at my pack of friends: Gilroy shrugged; Ivan shook his head slowly, looking very concerned; but Indigo was smiling.

"I know how to get the hogs into the pens," she said with a wink. "You might even say it's my specialty."

"How?" the three of us said in unison.

"We'll herd them in," she said.

We all looked at each other and then back at Indigo, not sure what to say. Finally, Gilroy said, "But we're sporting dogs; we don't know how to herd."

"No problem," she said. "I'm going to teach you. Meet me behind my house tomorrow afternoon for Herding 101."

CHAPTER 11

The next day on my rounds, I stopped by the Wisconsin memorial to look in on Chrisss and possibly ask him for a favor. I stepped into the woods a few feet toward the honeysuckle thicket and quietly called out, "Hello, Chrisss, are you around?"

"I'm here, Ranger," he replied, and a few moments later he slithered over to where I was standing. "It's nice to see you again, Thunder," he said politely.

"Has everything been going okay for you here, Chrisss? No more trouble I hope."

"I'm doing fine, Thunder—no more trouble at all. I've actually been quite comfortable here; it's like a vacation," he said.

"Chrisss, I was hoping to ask you for a favor. We have some wild hogs causing damage to park property. In a couple of days, my pack and I plan to herd them into the hog traps the rangers have placed around the park. We need to know where the hogs hang out so we can round them up. I thought perhaps someone with your natural stealth and your experience with vermin control might be able to help us."

"Say no more, Thunder," he said. "I'll have a full report ready for you tomorrow."

I thanked Chrisss and moved on with my rounds. I wanted to stop by the Grant statue to check on Seymour the skunk and his mother. I found them just inside the woods behind the clearing. Seymour greeted me enthusiastically.

"Thunder! Come look—we dug a new burrow right here under this magnolia tree," he said.

"It's lovely, really nice," I said.

"And some very nice squirrels came by and brought us a basket of nuts," Seymour's mother said. "Such hospitality!"

"I'm going to help Jerry and the other squirrels pass out some nuts tonight," Seymour said.

"That's very nice, Seymour. We do have a lot of extra animals here right now. I'm sure they can use the help."

* * *

Indigo lived just outside the park boundary line, so close that you could see the Texas state monument from her back yard. She said it was the perfect place to learn herding because there was plenty of wide open space in that part of the park and she could keep an eye on Tanisha at the same time. That afternoon, I trotted over from headquarters to find Ivan and Gilroy had already arrived and were eager to get started.

"Herding," Indigo explained, "is all about being smarter than the sheep. You have to stay one step ahead of them but never let them know you're ahead of them. Of course, that's all metaphorical, you know; you never actually get ahead of them— you have to pretty much stay behind them. Is that clear?"

Her question was met with blank stares from the three of us, who did not understand enough to even say yes or no. Finally, I raised my paw and said, "I'm from Texas. We don't have metaphors."

Indigo tried to explain again. "It's psychological, you see. You have to get them moving in the direction you want them to go but, at the same time, pretend that you don't care which direction they are going and that you have nothing to do with them—you just happen to be in the same pasture by coincidence."

There were more blank stares from the three of us. "Could you repeat that in Russian? I think

I might get it better in my native language," Ivan said.

Indigo giggled at that. "It helps if you can whistle or hum. Then you just hum a little tune while you pretend to be looking off in another direction. You know…doe deedoe deedoe deedoe deedoe. Don't worry, guys. You'll all catch on quickly," she assured us. "Any questions?"

Gilroy raised his paw and said, "What's a sheep? I thought we were gonna herd hogs."

It all seemed pretty complicated, but soon Indigo had us running some drills. "You run clockwise to turn them to the east," she said. "Always stay outside the herd. Never get mixed up with them—you'll split the herd, or you could get trampled."

We had been practicing for a couple of hours, and the sun was getting low in the sky over to the west behind the swollen Mississippi River. Some of the displaced deer had begun to come out of their thicket campsites to watch us practicing, and pretty soon the field began to feel like a sports arena with a cheering crowd of spectators. Tanisha had come outside to watch us practicing too. We could see her over in the backyard clapping her hands and yelling, "Good dogs! Good dogs!"

Some does walked over to Indigo and whispered something to her. "Great idea!" she said. "Guys, the does suggested we practice herding the little fawns." The giggling does stepped aside, and behind them were a half dozen adorable spotted fawns.

"Positions, everyone," called Indigo. We took up our positions behind and flanking the group of young deer. Indigo called out, "To me," and we started to creep in closer to get the herd moving. Slowly, we circled just like Indigo had taught us, but when we got too close, the fawns scattered in every direction at once.

"Bring in the outliers," Indigo called.

"They're all outliers," I hollered back as we vainly tried to gather the deer children back into a group. Every time we got two or three of them together, they would bounce around each other and take off in opposite directions. I approached a single fawn to move her back to the middle, but as I approached, she put her head down and tail up in the universal "I want to play" signal. "No time for play now. We're working," I said, but she just wagged her little white tail and bounded over me. I glanced over at the adult deer; they were falling over laughing at us. "Come on, guys! We've got to pull it together," I said. We regrouped and again started to round up the playful kids, but this time we had them together in a few minutes and moving toward the trees that Indigo had designated to represent the gate. As the last fawn walked through, Indigo and the adult deer broke into cheers.

"That was great!" said Indigo. "Now we are ready for Operation Pigs in a Blanket." But suddenly we were distracted by rustling in the underbrush behind us. As we watched, the same three pigs from yesterday stepped out of the woods and into the open field, too close for comfort to Indigo's back yard, where Tanisha was playing.

Indigo shoot across the battlefield like a cannonball, and I bolted after her with Ivan and Gilroy on my tail. Behind us, deer scattered in every direction, diving into the woods and thickets. I'm usually the fastest dog in the pack, but there was no catching Indigo. She flew over the fence, and with one last, long stride, she leapt in front of the gate, placing herself squarely between her family and the hogs. She bared her teeth and growled fiercely. "Back away from my little girl."

"Kinda touchy, aren't you?" the big sow squealed sarcastically. "Anyone would think you didn't want us to be hanging around your yard, playing with your sweet little human."

By that time, I had caught up and skidded to a halt next to Indigo. I growled my most menacing growl. Ivan appeared on my left and Gilroy on my right, both growling and barking at the hogs. Tanisha's mom heard all the commotion and looked out the back door. She screamed, ran outside and grabbed Tanisha up, and ran back to the house.

Faced with the four of us, the hogs stopped advancing, but they were still standing their ground and mouthing off. "Get out of here," I said. "You already had your warning."

"You're not being very neighborly, mister junior ranger," Quigley snorted. "What if we don't want to go?"

"Yeah, Ma said we could stay here until we turn this whole park into a big, muddy wallow," Delbert added.

"Back off! I'm not going to tell you again," Indigo snarled.

"Just what do you plan to do about it?" the sow challenged.

Indigo continued to growl and bark menacingly, and I knew we were seconds away from a big dirty fight with five hundred pounds of ham on the hoof when I heard Ranger Mike's truck on the tour road behind us. He was making his evening rounds to make sure all the visitors were out of the park before the gates were locked for the night. He pulled over when he saw us, hit the siren and the lights, and jumped out of his truck. "Hey, you hogs, get out of here," he hollered.

Caught by surprise, the hogs turned to run, but Quigley called back over his shoulder, "We'll be back!"

CHAPTER 12

Today is a big day at the park. Ranger Mike and I were leaving early for headquarters, so I was up and ready, waiting outside, when Spot strolled into the yard licking her whiskers.

"Where have you been all night?" I asked.

"Been doing some fishing," she said.

"You better be careful. The lower tier of the cemetery is flooded you know."

"I know. That's where I've been fishing."

"There could be all kinds of displaced animals down there—"

"There could be all kinds of displaced animals," she said mockingly. "I'm only interested in displaced fish...delicious displaced fish." She turned her tail to me and flicked the tip of it as she entered the house through the junior ranger door.

She's not a junior ranger, I was thinking as Ranger Mike opened the big door and reached down to pet Spot as their paths crossed in the doorway.

At the ranger meeting that morning, Ranger Mike told us that the river was predicted to crest at the highest point ever. To mark the occasion, we had planned a special artillery demonstration by the cannon crew. They were going to fire Old Whistler, a cannon so named because of the loud whistling sound it makes when fired. The whistling sound is caused by the rifling inside the cannon barrel. The cannon still stands guard in the same place where it has been for a hundred fifty years.

With the park full of displaced animals camped out all over the place, I had to get over to Old Whistler to make sure all the temporary residents knew what was about to happen. Artillery fire is loud, and I wouldn't want them to be scared, but I also wouldn't want a spontaneous deer and opossum stampede to break out. So I trotted to the overlook to pass along the information.

As I approached the bluff where the cannon sits, I could see there was a lot of activity in the area and a lot of animals scurrying around the cannon. Oh boy, this doesn't look good, I was thinking. This doesn't look good at all.

Seymour saw me coming and came running over to me. "Oh, thank goodness, you're here, Thunder. I was just coming to look for you."

"What's going on here?" I asked. "The cannon crew will be here soon. They're going to fire Old Whistler in a few minutes."

"They can't fire that cannon, Thunder! Jerry is inside!"

"What?"

"With so many animals to feed, it was really putting a strain on Jerry's reserves. He had to dip into the cannon storage to find enough nuts," Seymour explained.

"Jerry stores nuts in the cannons?" I asked with surprise.

"He said it was a handy place to keep a few nuts out of the weather. This morning he crawled down in the cannon barrel to pull out the last few nuts, and he got stuck."

"We've got to get him out right away, Seymour," I said. I hurried over to the cannon and put my face as far down the barrel as I could. "Jerry, are you in there?"

"No, I'm standing right behind you! Boo!" he said.

"Hold the jokes, Jerry. We've got to get you out right away. They're going to fire Old Whistler today, in just a few minutes."

"This cannon hasn't been fired in a hundred fifty years!" Jerry's protested, his voice echoing from the cannon barrel.

"But it's going to be fired today, and they'll be here any minute!" I said urgently.

"Thunder! I'm stuck in here! Do something!"

"I can't see you at all, Jerry. It's too dark," I said. "Wiggle your tail." I reached as far down the barrel as I could with my paw, but I felt nothing fluffy like a squirrel tail.

"Let me try, Thunder. I'm little. I can go down the barrel and try to pull him out," Seymour suggested.

"Good idea, Seymour. Give it a try."

"Here I come, Jerry.... Okay, I've got Jerry's tail.... Ugh...ugh...and I'm pulling as hard as I can, but he's still stuck."

From down the road, I could hear the drummers and the cannon crew marching this way. "They're coming—the cannon crew is coming!" some of the other squirrels shouted.

I've got to do something quick, I thought. I put my paws up on the cannon barrel. I could see the tip of Seymour's tail, and I remembered what he had told me about his spray being more or less automatic when someone grabbed his tail, but sometimes a ranger's got to do what a ranger's got to do.

"Hang on to Jerry, Seymour," I said. I grabbed

Seymour's tail in my mouth and pulled as hard as I could. Jerry and Seymour came flying out, and I fell back on my haunches with a big face full of skunk spray. "Ahhh! Yuck!" I snorted and spit for a moment, and then I finally managed to say, "Are you boys okay?"

"I'm okay," said Seymour.

"I may never be okay again," said Jerry. "For a little fella, you pack a powerful stink."

"Thank you," said Seymour. "That's quite a compliment to a skunk."

Seymour and the squirrels scurried off into the woods, and I headed back to headquarters. I had a lot to get done before the big roundup that night, and I really didn't have time for a side trip to the beauty parlor. But on the other hand, I wasn't going to be sneaking up on anybody without a bath in the anti-skunk shampoo, so I found Ranger Mike and gave him my most pathetic, sad puppy face. It worked—he pulled out the shampoo and started scrubbing.

"I hope you're not going to make a habit of this," he said.

After my bath, Ranger Mike and I went downtown to the riverfront to watch the hydrologists and engineers measure the official high water mark on the levee wall. The water level had reached 57.1 feet as the flood surge moved down the river and past the city on its way to the Gulf of Mexico. It was the highest water mark ever recorded in Vicksburg, almost a foot higher than the previous record set in 1927.

I was happy to see the high water mark set because that meant the flood water would begin to recede, and soon all the displaced animals would be able to return to their homes. But I still had the wild pigs to deal with, and they had sworn they wouldn't leave until they had turned the whole park into a giant hog wallow.

CHAPTER 13

I met my friends at the entrance that night determined to corral the dangerous and destructive feral hogs. I unfolded the park map I had brought and showed the others the locations of the three big hog pens. "All the hog pens are hidden in the woods," I said. "The first one is here near the Wisconsin state memorial, the second one is in the woods behind the Illinois monument, and the last one is in the woods just past the Cairo. As you know, that last one is close to my house, where the highway and the lower tier of the cemetery are flooded. So be careful over there—the water is four feet deep in some places. Chrisss the king snake has done some scouting for us, and he has a report about where the hogs are hiding."

"I have identified four groups of pigs," Chrisss began. "A group of six is behind the Illinois monument. There is another larger group of eight or more that stay down in the valley between the Wisconsin memorial and the earthworks at the turnoff for the Cairo. The other groups are less predictable. There were about a dozen that stayed just inside the park boundary in the woods beyond the cemetery, but with the lower tier flooded, they could be anywhere. That just leaves the three you have already had some trouble with—the big sow and her two sons. Those three roam all over the park leaving a trail of destruction behind, so there's no telling where you will encounter them tonight. Good luck, but be careful," Chrisss said. "I heard the big sow say the next time she sees you, she's going to trample you in the mud, Thunder. She's big enough to do it, and I wouldn't want her stomping on me with those big, sharp hooves of hers."

"Thanks, Chrisss, that was good work, and don't worry—I'll be careful," I said. "Okay, guys, here's the plan. Gilroy, Ivan, and I will take up sentry locations here, here, and here," I said pointing to the locations on the map. Indigo will rove between positions and act as the tactical logistics coordinator to address any technical issues that may arise from mechanical equipment failure. Any questions?"

Gilroy raised his paw and said, "Uh, Thunder, I think you're being too official."

"Oh, sorry," I said. "What I mean is, everybody go stand up on top of a hill, and holler when you see the hogs coming, and if they happen to get out

94

of the pen, Indigo will come to help you chase them back in."

"Oh," Gilroy said, nodding. "That's a good plan."

"Okay, everybody, remember the signal," I said. "When you see the hogs, bark two shorts and a long."

Everyone nodded, and we took off in opposite directions to take up our sentry posts. It wasn't very long before I heard Gilroy's loud, clear voice: "Ow, ow owwwwwww. Ow, ow, owwwwwww. Two shorts and a long—that was the signal! I ran as fast as I could over to Gilroy's position at the Illinois. Indigo was already there; she and Gilroy were crouched in the brush while six wild hogs gouged and dug with their hooves and snouts on a fresh piece of grass next to the one they had already ruined.

"We'll start from here and work our way around to the left. That will turn them toward the holding pen," Indigo whispered.

"Okay," Gilroy and I said in unison.

We started to move, but then we heard Ivan from across the valley at the Wisconsin: "Woof, woof wooooooof! Woof, woof, wooooooooof," Ivan barked.

"Oh no. Now what?" Gilroy asked with concern.

"You two can handle this. I'll go help Ivan," Indigo said. When she saw the concerned looks on our faces, she added, "You got this—just remember what I taught you," and she took off.

"Let's do this, Gilroy," I said.

Slowly, we crept out of the brush and moved to the left of the group of hogs. They started to shift their grubbing in the direction of the trap. We moved in closer and closer, staying low to the ground so that we wouldn't attract too much attention or scare them into sudden action. It was working—they were drifting in the direction we wanted. When the pigs got close to the trap, one got a whiff of the corn in the feeder and nosed his way through the gate. The others saw him eating and pushed and shoved their way into the trap too. They were so busy fighting over the bait that they had not even noticed they couldn't get back out by the time Gilroy and I trotted off to help Ivan and Indigo.

When we got to the top of the next hill, we could see that Ivan and Indigo were making progress with their batch of pigs, but it was a bigger group, and there were a couple of outliers. Indigo signaled to us to bring in the outliers; I took one, and Gilroy the other. Soon we had them moving toward that gate as well, and the bait did its trick to lure them the rest of the way into the holding pen.

When the last pig was in the pen, I said, "We better get back over to my area to see what's going on." We jogged over to the ridge above the Cairo that overlooks the Yazoo Valley, the place where I had met Seymour and where we had first seen the hogs the night of the stakeout.

The sky was clear, and in the distance, the floodwater sparkled in the moonlight, ironically beautiful in spite of the trouble it had caused for the many animals and people it had displaced. The grassy hillside was softly illuminated, as were the backs of the dozen or so hogs wallowing and rooting in the mud they had created.

"The hog trap is fifty yards over that way at the edge of the woods," I said.

Indigo sized up the pigs and offered us a few last-minute instructions. "This lot will be a challenge. There are at least a dozen of them and there may be a few more around out of sight, but there are four of us, and that's more than enough dogs to move this many. Just remember to keep your movements subtle and slow. Don't get them stirred up."

We crept down the hill slowly, keeping low to the ground and pausing frequently to look nonchalant. Indigo gave the signal to circle counter-clockwise, and the herd began to drift in the direction of the pen. There were so many of them though; they kept bumping into one another and bouncing off in kind of a ricochet effect. The herd started to break up and sprawl out. Indigo started to run back and forth behind the herd, challenging any of the pigs that were facing the wrong way. Once we got them close to the pen, they could smell the corn in the feeder inside, and the pigs forgot we were even there. They made a break for the pen, running through the gate one after the other until they were all inside. Oddly, they didn't seem bothered to be in the pen at all. There was plenty of food, and they were all snacking on corn, mingling, and drinking water from the big tub in the middle of the pen. It was what you would imagine a hog party to be like, except that there was no hog music for them to dance to.

"We made pretty short work of that. You guys herded like pros. I'm voting for all three of you to be honorary sheep dogs," Indigo said.

"Well, excuse me for interrupting the congratulating and the speechmaking, but Your Honors have done gone and locked up our kin in that there pig prison. Me and the boys don't take too kindly to that." We turned to find the big sow with Quigley and Delbert a few feet behind us, and they did not look happy.

"Get out of the park," I said. "You've had two warnings."

"It's our constitutional right to be here."

"You forfeited that right when you broke the rules and threatened other visitors." I took a small step forward. "You have to leave—now."

"There are only four dogs, Delbert," said Quigley. "Three and a half really."

Out of the corner of my eye, I could see Gilroy bristle at that remark. "Steady, boy," I whispered, but I really wasn't sure what I was going to do or say next.

"You're gonna need a few more dogs if you want us out of this park, mister junior ranger," Delbert sneered.

At that moment, a loud Scottish voice on the top of the ridge boomed out, "Luckily, he's got a few more doggies."

We looked up and saw Scottie and a half dozen of our classmates from the Vicksburg Canine Academy lined up atop the hill. Scottie shouted, "Charge!" and the whole pack came barreling down at top speed. The pigs were dumbfounded. Their mouths fell open for a brief moment, and then the big sow turned around to run as fast as she could in the opposite direction, knocking the other two off their feet in the process. Delbert and Quigley were squealing loudly and rolling around on the ground as they tried to get enough momentum to turn upright and get their feet back under them. When they finally managed to get up, they took off running after the big sow.

Indigo said, "Quick! We can pen them while they're distracted. Away to me, Thunder."

I heard Indigo's command and immediately began to move to the right so I could circle around the three pigs counter-clockwise, and Indigo moved in the opposite direction to cut off their escape. We met in front of the running swine, turning them back in the direction of the pen. We kept driving them until all three squealed through the gate and joined the rest of their family in the big holding pen.

"Look, Ma, there's corn feeders in here!" Quigley exclaimed greedily.

"Hey, save some for me," Delbert snorted.

Ivan, Gilroy, and the rest of our class joined us on the road. I looked over at Scottie and the rest of the pack, and I said, "Thanks, guys. Y'all really saved our bacon." We all fell down laughing for a few minutes.

"I heard about the pig trouble over behind Indigo's house yesterday," Scottie said. "When I heard signal barking tonight, I thought you might need a wee bit of assistance, so I barked up some friends, and we came a-running. You did a good job, Ranger Thunder. It was a smart idea to herd those dangerous beasts into the pens," Scottie said, and the rest of the pack nodded in agreement as they barked their congratulations.

"Thank you, guys," I said. "The four of us did it together, but Indigo deserves most of the credit. She had the idea to herd the hogs into the pens, and she taught us how to do the herding."

"Thanks, Thunder," Indigo said demurely. "It was really instinct you know; I just like to herd stuff."

"Spoken like a true herder, lass. You've got a good head on your shoulders," Scottie said. "But it's getting late, so now that you've all been rescued safe and sound, we better be getting back to our homes. The paper boys and the milkmen will be out soon, and they're gonna need barked at."

We all murmured our agreement and said

goodnight. Everyone headed off toward their homes in town, and I turned to walk the short distance to my house in the park. It had been a long day and a long night, and I was pretty tired, but I felt good about what we had accomplished. Then a faint noise stopped me in my tracks. I listened for a moment with one ear pricked for better reception.

"Meow," I heard faintly.

CHAPTER 14

Ugh, it's the cat, I thought, and I started to walk on, but something made me hesitate, so I waited to hear it again. There was something about that meow; it wasn't whiney or condescending like the meows I had previously heard from Spot. This one was different—forlorn with a subtle nuance of desperation. Suddenly, I realized—It's a distress meow. Spot must be in trouble! Sure, she's a big meanie, and she hid my squeaky duck on top of the refrigerator, but she's in my pack—so I turned to follow her cry for help.

I found her in the very back of the cemetery on the lower tier where the river had spilled over the highway, flooding the hallowed ground. She had a precarious perch on top of Old Douglass's tombstone, which was now surrounded by water. It was only a few feet from the upper tier, which was still dry, and I was sure even Spot could have swam over to dry ground. But it wasn't the thought of getting her pristine white fur wet that was stopping her. It was the six-foot gator waiting for her to give it a try. The gator had his nose up against the stone, and the two of them were locked in a stare-down. This kitty was in a real bad predicament. When she saw me approaching, she meowed, "Thunder, do something."

"Okay!" I said. "But what?" I saw the gravity of her situation, but I was at a loss as to how to help her, and I was hoping she would have an idea.

"I don't know," she meowed pitifully.

"Okay, don't panic," I said. "I'll think of something." Okay, I thought, what are my options? In a physical confrontation with a six-foot gator, I'd be no better off than she would be, so that was no good. I could poke him with a stick, and maybe he would chase me. I'm fast enough to get away from him on land, and Spot could get away while he was chasing me. I looked around on the ground for a tree branch or a long stick to poke the gator with, but the cemetery was meticulously maintained. I couldn't find a long stick or branch on the ground anywhere. But that gave me another idea.

There were no branches on the ground, but there were some in the tree overhead. A nearby oak tree had a big, wide canopy of leafy branches. One of the lower limbs stretched out above the tombstone where Spot was stranded. The limb was full of long, leafy branches that were small enough to be flexible but strong enough to allow a

five-pound cat to traverse to safety. I called over to Spot, "Get ready to make a jump for it!" as I pointed up at the branch with my nose and my paw.

She looked up, saw the branch I was pointing to, and nodded. "Ready," she said.

Just like grabbing an orange off the tree back home on the farm in Texas, I thought, and I jumped up as far as I could and caught hold of the tree branch with my teeth. I pulled it down a foot or two, and Spot jumped for it. She caught the branch, clinging to it with her front paws and claws; then she managed to wrap her hind legs around it as well. She hung there upside down below the branch for only a second or two before she was able to right herself. Then she ran up the branch and down the tree trunk a good thirty feet from the waiting gator. The gator thought about crawling out of the water to come after us, but instead, he just snapped his jaws shut with disgust and swam away.

Spot and I looked at each other for a few seconds. "Good boy," she finally said. Then she turned and ran for home.

"You're welcome," I called after her. I plodded home exhausted, entered through the junior ranger door, and headed straight for my bed. As I turned a couple of circles preparing to lay down,

I stepped on a lump under the blanket and heard a familiar "wak-wak" sound. Could it be? I nosed around in the corner, and yes, there he was—my squeaky duck had been returned. "I've missed you, buddy," I said, and I curled up with him and fell contentedly to sleep.

CHAPTER 15

In a week or so we began to notice the water level was starting to go down, and within a few more days, the river had vacated the cemetery and retreated back across the highway. Everyone was happy and relieved to see the landscape beginning to look familiar again. Most of the deer, squirrels, and other animals in the temporary camping facilities were preparing to return to their homes in the previously submerged thickets and treetops. Some were already gone.

I was still doing my best to be of assistance by consulting maps and making sure campsites were as clean on departure as they had been when the animals first arrived, tired and confused, a couple of weeks ago. I said goodbye to a few families every evening, wishing them well and encouraging them to visit the park again soon.

A few of the animals, like Seymour and his mother, had no practical way of returning to their homes upriver and were now facing a decision about the future. I made a point to go by Grant's statue and look in on the skunk family almost every day.

That was where I was headed this morning.

Along the way, I couldn't help but notice that it was going to be a particularly beautiful day. There was a little bit of pre-dawn mist hanging over the battlefield, which always makes for a spectacular sunrise. I arrived at the skunks' den just an instant before sunup to find Seymour outside also admiring the majestic pink and orange sky. We paused to watch as the first ray of sunlight broke over the horizon and, as if by magic, instantly burned off all the mist.

"I never get tired of watching that," I said.

"Neither do I," Seymour agreed. "Thunder, I'm glad you came by. I wanted to talk to you about something now that the river is going down and the flood is almost over. Mother and I love it here in the park, and we would like to stay on permanently. What do you say, Junior Ranger? Could you use a couple of more skunks in the park?"

"Of course, Seymour, you are welcome to stay. I know Jerry can always use another assistant, especially now that his stockpile of nuts is depleted. He's going to need a lot of help building it back up," I said.

"Great! I'm going to go ask him for the job right now!" Seymour exclaimed. "See you later,

Thunder," he said, and he scampered off to find Jerry.

He's a good skunk, I thought as I turned back toward the Cairo to finish my rounds. At the top of the ridge, a black snake with yellow speckles was curled up next to the path. "Good morning, Chrisss," I said.

"Thunder, look! The sandbar! I can see the sandbar out in the river," he said with excitement.

I looked out over the river, and sure enough, there was the big sandbar with two trees on one end and a big rock on the other, just as Chrisss had described it. "There it is. I see it," I said. "Now you can find your way back home."

"That's right," he said. "I've had a nice vacation here, but now I can't wait to get back to my job. There's no telling how many mice and rats have moved into the silo since I've been away. I waited to say goodbye to you, Thunder, so I could thank you for making me feel welcome here and for everything you did to help me."

"You're welcome, Chrisss, but there's no need to thank me. I'm a junior ranger, and I was just doing my job. Besides, you really helped out with the wild pig roundup.

"Happy I could help, Thunder," Chrisss said.

"It was a pleasure to get to know you, Chrisss. Come back to visit anytime. After all, the park belongs to all of us," I said.

Chrisss nodded, uncoiled himself, and said, "I better get going if I want to be home before dark. Bye, Thunder. Take care of yourself."

"So long, Chrisss. Safe travels." I watched as Chrisss slithered down the big hill and out to the edge of the river. He paused and turned his head back, I barked a last goodbye, and he slipped into the water and began swimming toward the sandbar. I was sad to see my new friend go, but at the same time, I was happy he could now find his way back home. I watched for a few minutes, and then I turned and trotted off toward headquarters.

CHAPTER 16

At last it was graduation day at the Vicksburg Canine Academy. I had worked hard to learn my obedience lessons, and that night Mrs. Katz would be testing me and the rest of the class in front of all our family and friends. I was excited that my mama and grandma would be coming to the graduation.

Ranger Mike and I arrived at the picnic pavilion to find Ivan and Gilroy were already there. I walked over, and we sniffed each other in greeting. "How's everything going at the park?" Ivan asked.

"It's going well," I said. "Chrisss went home a few days ago, but Seymour and his mother have decided to stay for good. Most of the other displaced animals have returned to their homes, but a few deer are still waiting for the mud to dry up a little more. The park is almost completely back to normal except for all the bare spots where the grass was uprooted by the pigs. The maintenance crew is working on it though, and if anybody can get the grass to grow back, it's them."

Indigo arrived with Tanisha and the rest of her family. She walked over to us. "I'm excited about graduation!" she said. "I'm so proud of Tanisha for learning how to teach me how to sit and stay."

We all snickered a little. "Yeah, that's what happened," I teased. "Indigo, you held your own leash most of the time."

"I know," she said, smiling, "but being together is what matters, not who's holding the leash." We all nodded our agreement.

Mrs. Katz was busy organizing the event. "Set up the stage right here," she said. "Put the podium on the left, and hang that bunting on the front of the stage. The diplomas...where are the diplomas?"

"Here they are. I've got them," one of her helpers said as she carried in a tray of scrolled parchment papers, each one tied with a blue ribbon.

"Oh, very good. Put them here on this table," Mrs. Katz instructed.

"What should I do with this big bowl of dog biscuits?" her assistant asked. I felt my ears prick up involuntarily as I strained to hear her reply.

"Put them on the picnic table there with the liverwurst and rawhide chews."

Liverwurst, rawhide, and dog biscuits! This

is going to be some party, I thought as Mrs. Katz called the class to order.

"Attention, class. Our guests will be arriving soon. I want you all to wait over there with your partner until the guests are seated. When the music starts, walk with your partner down the center aisle, and sit in the front row to wait for your turn. I will call each of you up on to the stage in alphabetical order. You will perform the basic moves we have learned on my command. If you do well, you will receive your diploma."

Ranger Mike and I walked with the others over to the designated area to wait for the ceremony to begin. I greeted Scottie and some of my other classmates with a friendly sniff. We watched the guests as they arrived and found their seats. There was a general buzz of excitement and anticipation in the air. I scanned the crowd for my family. There they were, my mama and my grandma, sitting in the third row on the left. I can't wait till it's my turn. I want to show my mama what a good ranger I am.

As we waited, I thought Gilroy was starting to look a little nervous. "Hey, Gilroy, you got this, buddy," I said. "You stood up to some big ol' mean wild hogs. This will be a cakewalk for you, pal."

He smiled. "Thanks, Thunder. I needed

that," he said. He took a deep breath and started to look a little more relaxed.

Mrs. Katz stepped up to the podium. "Welcome, family and friends of the Vicksburg Canine Academy obedience class." The music began to play, and we straightened up our line, marched into the pavilion down the center aisle, and took our seats in the front row. Mrs. Katz called out, "Bella." Bella, the bulldog, took the stage. "Sit," said Mrs. Katz, and then "Down," "Stay," and "Heel." Bella performed beautifully. "Shake," said Mrs. Katz. Bella held out her paw to shake hands, Mrs. Katz briefly took her paw in a friendly handshake, and then she offered Bella her diploma. Bella took the diploma in her mouth and walked proudly off the stage.

That didn't look too bad, I thought as Mrs. Katz called the next student. But the thing about having a name like Thunder, which comes near the end of the alphabet, is that you have a long time to think before your turn. While I was watching my classmates taking their final exams, part of my brain was thinking up things that could go wrong. I could trip on the stairs…I could have to go pee…I could forget my own name and miss my turn. Stop thinking that way, I told my brain, you're making me nervous, and when I get nervous, I forget things. I could forget how to sit...wait...what is sit? I forgot what that word means!

"Thunder," called Mrs. Katz.

My turn already? Shakily, I stood up and started walking to the stage with Ranger Mike. My stomach hurts. I feel sick. Why did I have to sneak a few bites of grass while we were waiting? We mounted the stairs and stepped up on the stage. She's going to say something any second now. Thunder, do something! I'd heard that a lot lately, but I was saying it to myself this time. I looked out over the crowd—there was my mama and my grandma smiling at me. In the front row, all of my friends and classmates were smiling their encouragement, especially Gilroy. Gilroy had performed his test flawlessly. That's it! I thought. I'll take a little of my own advice. I took a deep breath and reminded myself of everything I had accomplished over the past couple of weeks. I had helped a lot of displaced animals, I had protected the park from the greedy pigs who wanted to turn the whole thing into their own private hog wallow, and I had worked hard preparing for this very test. Yeah, that was me! I got this! Bring it, Mrs. Katz!

"Thunder, sit," commanded Mrs. Katz. I sat. She patted me on the head and said, "Good boy." I completed the rest of my test perfectly, and Mrs.

Katz smiled broadly as she shook my paw and handed me my diploma. I was proud of myself as I carried my diploma carefully in my mouth across the stage and back to my seat with Ranger Mike.

"Congratulations, graduates! Everyone is invited to stay for refreshments, but first I have one more presentation to make," said Mrs. Katz. "Gilroy, please come forward." Gilroy, smiling shyly, walked back to the stage with Connor. Mrs. Katz was holding out a small yellow vest, which she held up for everyone to see. "Gilroy, you have now completed the last step in your certification as a service dog. Congratulations!" She put the vest on Gilroy and fastened the strap around his chest. On the side of the vest, the words SERVICE DOG were printed in big black letters.

I ran over to congratulate Gilroy. "Gilroy, you're official now!" I said with excitement.

"Thanks, Thunder," Gilroy said, grinning ear to ear. Ivan was there patting Gilroy on the back, and Indigo brought Tanisha over to pet Gilroy and to meet Connor. It was a really fun party. We chowed down on treats and drank from a big punch bowl Mrs. Katz had filled with water.

I ran over to my mama, and she started kissing me on one side and my grandma was kissing me on the other. "Come on, Mama, Grandma, I want you

to meet all my friends, and then I want to show
you all around the park!"

"I'm so proud of you, son," my mama said,
and that made my chest swell out even more.

Made in the USA
Columbia, SC
22 April 2021